Care Bears™

Caring and Sharing

By Samantha Brooke
Illustrated by Jeff Harter

ISBN-13: 978-0-439-89468-5
ISBN-10: 0-439-89468-9
CARE BEARS ™ © 2007 Those Characters From Cleveland, Inc.
Used under license by Scholastic Inc. All rights reserved. Published by Scholastic Inc.
SCHOLASTIC and associated logos are trademarks and/or registered trademarks of Scholastic Inc.
12 11 10 9 8 7 6 5 4 3 2 1   7 8 9 10/0
Printed in the U.S.A.
First printing, April 2007

It takes caring and sharing to make friendships
blossom, and Care Bears do it in their own special way.

Bedtime Bear shows how much he **cares** about his friends by making sure they always have the sweetest dreams.

Share Bear thinks that sharing is fun. She likes giving her friends special treats — and she never leaves anyone out.

Champp Care Bear shows how much he cares about his friends by reminding them that they are all winners.

Love-a-lot Bear knows that sharing a little love goes a long way! She always remembers to tell her friends how much she loves them.

Funshine Bear cares about his friends by showing them that any time can be fun time — all you need are your friends and a little imagination.

Cheer Bear is always ready to share a smile that will brighten her friends' day. If they are down, Cheer Bear will lift their spirits.

Tenderheart Bear is the King of Kindness. He thinks that **sharing** a hug can sometimes be the best medicine.

Laugh-a-lot Bear is the Queen of Giggles. She knows that sharing laughter with her friends will chase away gloomy clouds.

Grumpy Bear knows what it's like to have the rainy day blues.
He shows how much he cares about his friends by being a good listener.

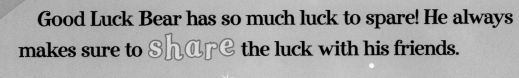

Good Luck Bear has so much luck to spare! He always makes sure to $share$ the luck with his friends.

How do you show your friends that you *care* about them?